MIDDLESBROUGH LIBRARIES & INFORMATION

3 1 AUG 2012
1 4 SEP 2016

D1313020

009042216 3

Middlesbrough Libraries

First published in Great Britain in 2010 by
ANDERSEN PRESS LIMITED,
20 Vauxhall Bridge Road, London SW1V 2SA
www.andersenpress.co.uk
www.barbaramitchelhill.com

All rights reserved. No part of this publication may be reproduced,
stored in a retrieval system or transmitted in any form, or by any
means, electronic, mechanical, photocopying, recording or
otherwise, without the written permission of the publisher.

The rights of Barbara Mitchelhill and Tony Ross to be identified as
the author and illustrator of this work have been asserted by them
in accordance with the Copyright, Designs and Patents Act, 1988.

Text © Barbara Mitchelhill, 2010
Illustration © Tony Ross, 2010

British Library Cataloguing in Publication Data available.

ISBN 978 184 939 035 4

Printed and bound in Great Britain by
CPI Bookmarque, Croydon CR0 4TD

*For Maisy. A great football fan
and Stoke supporter.*

Chapter 1

My name is Drooth. Damian Drooth, ace detective. I search out crimes in all kinds of places.

Take last Saturday. Mum was running the café at the Rangers' football ground – which was cool cos I got in free and could watch the match. Brilliant. It was a big match. A sell-out. So I arranged to meet Winston, Harry and Tod inside the gate at one o'clock.

But when I got there, I could only see Harry and Tod.

'Where's Winston?' I asked. 'He's not usually late for a match.'

'Dunno,' said Tod.

Just then Harry's mobile rang and he was soon deep in conversation. When he'd finished, he turned and said, 'It's bad news. They won't let Winston into the ground.'

'Why?' I asked.

'It's his ticket,' said Harry. 'They say it's a forgery.'

I was gobsmacked. Who would go around forging tickets? I'd never heard anything so crazy.

'You can make a fortune doing forgeries,' said Tod, who watches the History Channel a lot. 'People forge famous paintings and stuff and earn millions.'

'Mmmm,' I said. 'But who would forge a ticket for a match? And . . .

where did Winston get it from?'

'All the tickets were sold out but there was a man outside the ground who told Winston he'd got some for sale.'

'And he bought one?'

'Yes.'

Sometimes I despair. How could Winston buy a ticket from a ticket tout? A real crook. Winston was part of my Detective School, wasn't he? He should know better.

'Where's Winston now?' I asked.

'He's outside,' said Harry, pointing to the gate. 'He hasn't got any money to buy another ticket.'

'Leave it to me,' I said, tapping my nose. 'I have a plan.'

Luckily Mum had asked me to fetch a gateau out of the van. This couldn't be better.

PLAN Part 1:

I ran to the gate where Mr Thomas was checking the tickets. (He used to be a footballer and now he has a bad back and not much hair.) He knows me cos I always came to help Mum in the café.

'Hello, Damian,' he said. 'Looking forward to the match?'

'Sure thing,' I said. 'But I've got to go out to the van first.'

'Righto, son,' he said, patting me on the shoulder. 'You go ahead.' And he let me through.

So far, so good. Outside the ground I soon spotted Winston pacing up and down Cranberry Street. He was looking as miserable as a worm on a hook.

'Over here, Win,' I shouted, and beckoned him towards the van, which was parked in the road. He cheered up when I told him my plan.

I unlocked the back door and reached inside.

'Grab hold of this,' I said and passed him a massive chocolate gateau with cream in the middle and chocolate sprinkles on top. Then I took another one.

PLAN Part 2:

We went back to the gate where Mr Thomas looked longingly at Mum's cakes.

'Ah,' he said. 'You're helping out at the café, are you? Good boys!'

We smiled and nodded as we walked straight through the gate. The simple ideas are always the best, that's what I say.

End of Plan

Unfortunately, there was a crush of people near the gate. Thwack! Splodge! Winston's chocolate gateau was flattened against his Rovers' sweatshirt, which was a shame as it was brand new.

'What will you tell your mum, Damian?' said Tod, who was waiting nearby.

'She won't be pleased to see the remains of that gateau,' said Harry.

'No probs,' I said. 'I won't take it. She only asked me to fetch one anyway, and she won't even remember there were two in the van.'

I'm sure you'll agree that there was no point in wasting the squashed gateau, so we scraped most of it off Winston's shirt and shared it. As a matter of fact, chocolate gateau has an amazing effect on my brain. It always puts it into top gear. It wasn't long before I had worked out a plan for catching the fraudster who had sold the forged ticket.

Chapter 2

It was almost time for the kick off. The four of us went to find our seats. Mine was next to a girl called Annabelle Harrington-Smythe who goes to our school and is OK – for a girl. Long hair, blue eyes, that kind of thing.

'Hello, Damian,' she said. 'Not catching any criminals today?'

'As a matter of fact, I am,' I said. 'A major crime has just been committed and I intend to solve it.'

Dixie Stanton, Annabelle's friend, was sitting next to her. She started giggling. She's always giggling. She's a real pain.

Annabelle ignored her. 'What does this criminal look like?' she asked.

Winston had given me some details and I had made notes in my detective's notebook.

'He's tallish with a sort of stubbly chin,' I said, flicking through my notebook. 'You know the type. It's as though he hasn't shaved for a week. In my experience, this is the worst kind of criminal.'

I think Annabelle was dead interested. She asked loads of questions.

'What was he wearing, Damian?' she asked and leaned forward to get a look at my notes.

Winston butted in. 'A woolly cap, a football scarf, jeans, a black jacket . . .'

'You see, Annabelle,' I interrupted, 'to a fully trained detective like me, it's obvious that he's a football fan and he'll come to watch the match. He could even be sitting near us. You never know,' I said darkly.

'OK. So how will you spot him in this crowd?' asked Dixie Stanton, who was just trying to be clever – which she is NOT.

'As a matter of fact,' I said, 'I've already got my plan.'

It was this: after the match, Tod and Harry would go to one gate. Winston would go to the other. Then, as the crowd left the ground, they would look out for the forger. Unfortunately, I would not be there as I had to go and help Mum. Worst Luck!

'Can we help?' asked Annabelle. 'The more of us, the better.'

'I'm great at karate,' said Dixie Stanton.

Of course, I had to turn down their offer. 'We can manage, thanks,' I said.

'This is real detective work and Tod, Harry and Winston have been attending my detective school for ages.'

Annabelle, who has a very nice smile, said, 'Well, if you need our help, Damian, just ask.'

Winston frowned and dug me in the ribs. 'We don't need girls, do we?'

And I had to agree.

When the match was over (nil-nil . . . *dead depressing*), I rushed up to the café to do my jobs as fast as I could. Mum was in a bad mood.

'I know I put two gateaux in the van, Damian,' she said, narrowing her eyes and glaring at me. 'What happened to the other one?'

I smiled my best innocent smile – showing all my teeth and everything. 'Maybe you just *thought* you brought two gateaux, Mum. Your memory's not brilliant, is it?'

'MY MEMORY IS PERFECTLY ALL RIGHT!' she shouted. 'If it wasn't in the van, where has it gone, Damian?'

At this point, I dropped a jug full of milk and she was too busy being mad with me about that to worry about the gateau.

'Right,' she said when she'd mopped up the milk, 'carry those dishes out to the van. CAREFULLY.'

This is the worst part about being a boy, if you ask me. I was on the trail of a master criminal and, instead of catching him, I was forced to do boring jobs. It was a complete waste of my brilliant brain power.

A whole thirty minutes passed before I could meet up with the gang.

'What's the news?' I asked.

'Nothing,' said Tod, shuffling his feet and looking miserable. 'There were loads of men in woolly hats and scarves but they weren't the forger.'

14

'Maybe he wasn't in the football crowd,' said Harry.

I couldn't help wondering whether if I hadn't been at the café doing jobs for Mum, I would have spotted him.

'We need ideas,' I told the gang. 'Let's get some chips before we go home. Chips are great for the brain.'

'Are they?' asked Tod, who always likes to know the facts.

'I read it somewhere,' I lied, and headed across Cranberry Street to the chip shop where a long queue of football fans was forming. I spotted Annabelle standing in the middle of it.

(Unfortunately she was with Dixie Stanton.)

'Hello, Damian,' Annabelle called. 'Found your criminal?'

'Gathering information,' I said as we marched past and joined the back of the queue.

We had been standing there for a couple of minutes when Winston suddenly yelled, 'Look! That's him!' He was pointing down Cranberry Street towards a tall man in a scruffy black jacket who was coming out of Mr Maxwell's newsagent's shop.

At last! We were on the trail of the ticket fraudster.

Chapter 3

We left the queue immediately.

'Right,' I said. 'We'll follow him. We might find out where he lives.'

We kept several paces behind the crook and I noted that he had dirty trainers and walked with his shoulders hunched. A typical criminal!

Annabelle had followed us with Dixie Stanton tagging on behind.

'Can we help?' she asked.

'No thanks,' I replied. 'I think I've got it all wrapped up.'

Dixie Stanton tried to butt in. 'Go on. Let me give him a karate chop!' she said.

But I just ignored her.

'Your loss, Damian,' she said. As if I cared!

When the fraudster came to the corner, he turned right. This was getting dead exciting. Unfortunately, he had parked his car in the next street and, before I knew it, he jumped inside and drove off. I wondered if he knew we were on his trail.

But all was not lost. I had my detective's notebook and I did a brilliant sketch of him.

'So what now?' Tod asked.

I was ready with my next move. 'We take this drawing of the fraudster to Mr Maxwell's shop,' I said, showing them my notebook.

'That drawing's rubbish, Damian,' Tod said. 'You can't identify anybody from that.'

But the others thought it wasn't that bad so we headed back down the road to the newsagent's where Mr Maxwell was on the pavement outside smoking a cigarette. In my opinion, this is a bad example to other people.

I stood in front of him, holding up the picture so he could see it. 'This man came into your shop a few minutes ago,' I said. 'Do you know who he is?'

Mr Maxwell took the fag out of his mouth and shook his head. 'Never seen him before in my life,' he said and put the cigarette back in again. But, if you ask me, he hadn't even glanced at the picture.

'Take another look,' I said. (This is what detectives always say when they are interviewing people. I've seen it loads of time on TV.)

'Leave off, Damian,' he said. 'I'm busy.' And he dropped his fag on the pavement (disgusting!) and went back inside the shop.

'What now?' asked Tod *again*.

'The only thing to do,' I said, 'is to tell Inspector Crockitt about the forged tickets and show him the picture. He'll be dead interested.'

So we legged it down to the police station where PC Nobbs was on the desk. I knew him from other crimes I had solved.

I slapped my notebook in front of him and said, 'I have some information for Inspector Crockitt. It involves a major criminal.'

PC Nobbs leaned over the desk and frowned. 'I'm afraid the Inspector is busy, Damian,' he said. But I knew this was not true. Inspector Crockitt is never too busy to see *me*.

I hate making a fuss but it was the only thing I could do. I got the gang to chant:

What do we want?
Inspector Crockitt!
When do we want him?
NOW!

Suddenly, doors started opening and police came rushing into reception, thinking there was a riot going on. And when Inspector Crockitt burst from his office, PC Nobbs looked mega embarrassed and his cheeks turned as red as a ripe tomato.

'Ah, Damian!' the Inspector said. 'I could have guessed it was you.'

I turned to the gang. 'See,' I said. 'I told you Inspector Crockitt would be expecting me.'

Chapter 4

Things at the station didn't turn out well. Inspector Crockitt was not in a good mood. He could charge us with disturbing the peace, he said. Then we would all have a criminal record.

'I'm off,' said Tod. 'My mum would kill me if she found out.'

'Me too,' said Harry.

And even Winston said he had to dash back to feed his guinea pig.

So that just left me with Inspector Crockitt, face to face. I explained about the case I was working on. I opened my notebook and showed him my drawing.

'This,' I said, 'is the man who sold the forged tickets.'

'Mmm,' said Inspector Crockitt. 'That's not much help, I'm afraid. Now if you had a photograph – that would be different.'

'I can describe him,' I said, helpfully.

Inspector Crockitt sighed. He looked tired to me. 'Right then, Damian,' he said. 'You'd better write a statement about what happened.'

He gave me a form to fill in and then he left me to get on with it. I wrote everything down. Best handwriting. Best spelling. Everything.

What did Inspector Crockitt do while I was slaving away? He rang my mum, that's what. Can you believe it? She came rushing down to the station.

She was not pleased.

'I'm very sorry that Damian has wasted your time, Inspector,' she said. 'He quite often plays at being a detective. He's very imaginative, you know. Always seeing trouble when there isn't any. But I'll make sure he doesn't bother you again.'

I was shocked! How many crimes did I have to solve before she treated me like a professional? This was out of order. When we got home, she even sent me up to my room.

Anyway, I didn't waste any time. I went into organisation mode, preparing for a crime-busting day tomorrow. If the police wouldn't help to track down the fraudster, I would have to do it myself, as usual. Using Mum's mobile, I rang round all the trainee detectives. They had to come to the shed at ten o' clock the next morning. There was going to be an *emergency* meeting.

Chapter 5

The next day was Sunday. Brilliant! I usually woke to the smell of a real breakfast. Bacon and egg and fried bread. My favourite. But that Sunday, there was nothing and no sign of Mum in the kitchen.

This was bad news as I had to make my own breakfast – cereal (two bowls), four slices of toast with marmalade, a few cold sausages and some baked beans I'd found in the fridge.

After this disappointing start to the day, I hurried down to the shed, ready for the meeting. My plan was to write some leaflets and push them through the doors of every house near the football ground. I would do the drawing and the others could do the writing.

I'd been sitting on the old beer crate for half an hour by myself, when Winston walked in with Thumper (who smells really bad).

'Better late than never,' I said, spreading my notes on the plank we use for a table. 'Take a look at my leafllets.'

But Winston didn't seem interested. 'Can't stay,' he said. 'Dad only let me out cos I said the dog needed a walk. I've got to go back home. Gran's coming.'

This was bad news. 'What about the others?'

'Harry stays in bed till twelve on Sundays. Tod and Lavender have gone off to the seaside.'

My stomach sank as I realised I would have to track down the criminal and solve the crime alone.

But before he left, Winston gave me some important news. 'Guess what,' he said.

'What?'

'Annabelle What's-her-name took a photo of that ticket tout yesterday. You know, when he was getting in his car. She's got a camera on her mobile phone.'

I was amazed.
'Why didn't
she tell me?'
I said. 'She's
been withholding
information.'
Winston
shrugged. 'You
said you could
solve this case
yourself, remember.'

That was a fair comment. But things were different now she had a crucial piece of evidence. I had to see it.

'Ring her on her mobile,' said Winston and he handed me a scrap of paper with a number written on it.

I don't like involving girls in investigations – but needs must. I pulled Mum's mobile out of my pocket and tapped in Annabelle's number.

Chapter 6

I arranged to meet Annabelle round the back of the fish and chip shop down Cranberry Street. There was a row of garages there, crumbling and in a bad state.

'We use one of them for our gang hut,' she'd explained on the phone.

It was the first I'd heard of it.

She'd also told me she had printed the photo and pinned it up in the garage. This was brilliant news. I'd set off to meet her, determined to save my reputation as a prime detective.

I was walking down the road towards the park when I saw Inspector Crockitt. He was wearing plain clothes* and walking his dog, Peaches. I guess he hadn't seen me because he hurried through the park gate.

*Plain clothes are what police wear when they are not wearing uniform. Sometimes this means they are pretending to be somebody else to catch criminals.

Anyway I raced after him to say hello.

'Hello, Inspector Crockitt,' I called. I had to repeat it so many times that I wondered if his hearing was failing.

When he finally stopped and turned round, I noticed that he didn't look very cheerful. He was probably worrying about the level of crime in the area.

'Hello, Damian,' he said.

I stood close to him and spoke in my loudest voice to make sure he could hear. 'I THOUGHT YOU OUGHT TO KNOW,' I said.

'No need to shout, Damian,' he said. 'What is it?'

'I'm on the trail of that ticket fraudster.'

He frowned and then he sighed. 'Good. You carry on but don't go upsetting anybody, Damian. It's my day off.' Then he walked away.

I'm often surprised by the attitude of our police force. They shouldn't rely on a boy detective to solve local crimes. What does my mum pay her taxes for? That's what I want to know.

I walked out of the park and soon reached the row of shops on Cranberry Street. Only Mr Maxwell's newsagent's was open and I don't think they were busy because Mr Maxwell was leaning against the wall smoking a fag again. Does he ever stop? I think he was born with a cigarette in his mouth. It's disgusting.

I managed to sneak behind the shops without Mr Maxwell seeing me. This was where the old garages stood – well not exactly *stood*. They were nearly falling down and covered in graffiti. And there was litter everywhere.

There was no sign of Annabelle so I decided to search for the evidence myself. If I broke into the garage and found it, I needn't involve her.

I trained my expert eye along the row of wrecked buildings to find out which was her hideout. I soon spotted something sprayed on the door of the middle garage. This was the clue.

THE GARAGE GANG
RULES OK!

I hurried over, and tried to open the door but the hinges were so rusty that I could only open it a little way. So I squeezed through the gap but I got stuck halfway and had to wriggle to get inside. My jeans tore in a couple of places but, hey! they were only my second-best pair.

It was dark in the garage. The window at the back was covered in dirt and the only bit of light was coming from under the door. But when my eyes got used to the dark, I was able to look around.

Annabelle's gang had obviously been there. There were four stools, plenty of boxes, some girls' magazines and a few empty plastic lemonade bottles. Along one wall there was a long shelf stacked with old cans of paint. But best of all, pinned in the middle of the wall, was the photograph of the criminal. It was brilliant! You could even see the numberplate on his car. This was PROOF. I would take it at once to Inspector Crockitt.

Chapter 7

I took the photo off the wall but, before I could sneak out, I heard footsteps coming towards the garage.

'Damian! Are you in our gang hut?' It was Annabelle.

'I bet he's trying to pinch that photo. I'll thump him!'

Oh no! Dixie Stanton was with her.

My heart sank into my trainers. Now two girls were trying to get in on my detective work. That was gross. I decided that the best thing was to keep quiet. If I said nothing and hid behind some boxes, they might go away.

But I think Annabelle guessed I was inside. 'We were going to help you,' she said, 'but if you're going to be silly, we won't.'

She wasn't going to trick me into revealing my whereabouts. No way! I just kept silent.

'Be like that then,' yelled Dixie and she slammed the door of the garage shut. Now it was pitch black in there. Was I going to be stuck there for the rest of the day? Or maybe the rest of the week? I would be inside this grotty garage with no food and no drink. It was a nightmare.

'OK,' I yelled. 'Joke! Joke! I was here all the time.'

Luckily they opened the garage door and let me out.

Phew! It was good to see sunlight.

Annabelle stood in front of me with her hand outstretched. 'Give me my photograph,' she said.

'I'm taking it to Inspector Crockitt,' I replied, holding it behind my back. I wasn't going to give it up that easily.

'Give it to me,' she insisted.

'Give it up or else!' Dixie shouted as she stepped forward.

It was bad luck that a gust of wind suddenly whipped the photo out of my hand and tossed it in the air. We watched as it fluttered past the garages and finally fell by the fence where there were heaps of litter and patches of nettles. Unfortunately the photo was somewhere in the middle of the nettles.

'You did that on purpose!' yelled Dixie Stanton.

'I did not.'

'Then go and get it,' she said, coming closer and holding her hands towards me like a pair of weapons. She looked vicious and I didn't want to be on the receiving end of a karate chop.

'OK,' I said. 'I'll fetch it. No sweat.'

I took my time reaching the fence.

'Go on,' said Dixie, who was right behind me. 'Pick it up. You're not scared of a few nettles, are you?'

Of course I wasn't. I pulled my sleeve down to cover my hand and bravely reached among the rubbish.

The nettles were vicious. They must have been the strongest nettles in the world – if not the universe. They stung my hand. They stung my arm through my sweater. But I wasn't going to let Dixie Stanton see that I was in agony. No way. I just squeezed my eyes tight and bit my lip before reaching for the photo.

'Give it here,' she said – not even noticing I was in terrible pain.

I lifted my blistered hand and passed the photo to Annabelle.

'What's this, Damian?' she said. 'This isn't the photo.'

She was right. It was too small. I looked more closely and saw it was a ticket for a Rangers' match.

There was loads of litter by the fence. Was it any wonder I'd picked up the wrong piece of paper?

I turned round again, gritted my teeth and plunged my throbbing arm back among the nettles once more. This time I grabbed a handful of papers, hoping that one would be the photograph. The girls watched me like hawks as I kneeled down and spread the papers on the ground. There it was. Right in the middle. The snapshot of the criminal.

But Annabelle's blue eyes were fixed on me. 'That's odd,' she said. 'Most of these are tickets for the Rangers. How come?'

I hadn't a clue but I soon noticed that they all had the same number stamped on the bottom. I was immediately suspicious.

'I think,' I said as I stood up, 'I think we have just stumbled upon a major crime.'

Chapter 8

'What are you saying, Damian?' Annabelle asked.

'I'm saying that I think these tickets are forgeries and were printed somewhere near here.'

I could tell she was shocked. 'Why would anyone want to forge tickets for the Rovers' matches?'

She was a typical girl. She didn't understand the criminal mind.

'Money,' I explained. 'It would be dead cheap to print these. Then the forgers sell them and make a fortune.'

'Of course!' said Dixie Stanton. 'What a scam.'

I looked at the forgeries and it didn't take long for my brain to come up with a solution.

'These could have been blown from the forger's hideout,' I said. 'I'm going to take a look at the garages. One of these would be perfect for a hideout.'

Every garage in the row had a small window at the back, which I would be able to look in. I squeezed between the fence and the back walls of the garages and felt the nettles sting my legs in spite of my jeans. Sometimes, detective work can be seriously painful.

Most of the windows were filthy and were either cracked or broken. Only one was whole. It was the middle garage and its window was covered with a dark curtain.

My detective's alarm went off in my head. Why would anyone put a curtain up in an old wreck of a garage? Whoever owned it didn't want anybody to look in. They were obviously up to no good. I turned and pushed my way back through the weeds once again.

'I think I've found it,' I said, pointing to the middle garage – which was right next to Annabelle's own headquarters.

It was at that moment that Winston arrived with Thumper. I was very surprised.

'I thought you had to stay in cos of your gran?' I said.

Winston grinned. 'Yeah but Gran wanted to talk to Mum,' he said. 'You know. A chat. I kept interrupting and Mum got a bit annoyed.'

'So they asked you to take the dog for a walk?'

'Right,' said Winston, giving me one of his winks. 'I thought you'd be here.'

I filled him in on the crime I had uncovered.

'I reckon the forger works from here,' I said, tapping the middle garage. 'But we need to open it up.'

Unfortunately there was a massive padlock on the door.

'I can do it,' said Annabelle and she pulled a clip out of her hair and started picking at the lock. I have to admit, she was quick for a girl. She soon had it open.

So far so good. But as I opened the door, the most ear-splitting noise started up. One thing I hadn't expected – the garage had been fitted with a burglar alarm!

Chapter 9

Thumper started pulling on his lead and barking at the alarm. I dashed in to turn it off – but not before I'd spotted a *printing machine* and stacks of *paper*.

But not only that . . .

There were *more* forged tickets. Loads and loads of them on the bench.

'Geronimo! I was right,' I yelled to the others. 'This is where the forger works.'

Just then the wind whipped into the garage and the tickets swirled like snowflakes in a blizzard and flew out the door. They scattered everywhere and some of them dropped to the ground with the rest of the litter.

The alarm was still ringing.

'Turn it off, Damian,' Dixie Stanton yelled. 'We're going to be in dead trouble.'

I looked but there was no sign of a switch.

'We'd better run for it,' Winston yelled. 'Come on.'

But it was too late. Mr Maxwell from the newsagent's came dashing round the corner and up to the garage door.

'What are you kids up to?' he shouted, taking his fag out of his mouth and waving his arms like crazy.

This got Thumper excited and he growled and barked and strained at his lead until Winston couldn't hold him. And when Thumper lunged at Mr Maxwell, he sent the old man staggering backwards and crashing to the ground. There was a lot of swearing from Mr M and plenty of barking from Thumper.

'Sorry about the dog, Mr Maxwell,' I shouted as he lay there. 'But I've found something in that garage. I think there's criminal activity going on.'

I thought he'd be interested but he didn't seem to be. Perhaps the fact that Thumper was standing on his chest had something to do with it.

Then Winston suddenly pointed to smoke pouring out of the garage. Mr Maxwell must have dropped his cigarette when he fell. As I've said before, cigarettes are dangerous.

'Can I use your phone, Annabelle?' I asked and I dialled 999.

Two police cars arrived in seconds. Very impressive. But it turned out that it was nothing to do with my phone call. Someone had reported the alarm going off earlier.

'Oh, it's you,' said a policewoman as she jumped out of the car. 'What are you up to *this* time?'

It was PC Honey. We'd met before.

'I'm taking care of local crime,' I said.

'Causing it more like,' she snapped as she marched towards Mr Maxwell and dragged Thumper away from him.

I tried to tell her about my amazing detective work but she was too busy keeping a crowd of neighbours from getting too close to the fire. They had come to watch the excitement.

Soon I heard the siren of the fire engine coming down the road. It was only just in time as the flames were leaping higher and spreading. Now Annabelle's headquarters were in danger of going up in smoke too.

Just as the fire brigade started jetting their water onto the building, Inspector Crockitt arrived with his dog, Peaches. He must have heard all the noise on his way back from the park.

I rushed up to him at once. 'I've discovered a crime scene,' I told him.

'Have you indeed?' he said, heading towards PC Honey.

'Yes,' I said. 'But you needn't have come. It's your day off. Everything's under control.'

'I don't think so, Damian,' he said. Then he pulled a phone out of his pocket and dialled.

Chapter 10

After that, it got a bit out of hand. Mr Maxwell's wife suddenly appeared round the corner and went mad when she saw her husband lying on the floor.

'Leave him alone,' she yelled, grabbing a piece of wood and rushing over to strike Inspector Crockitt.

But Dixie caught Mrs Maxwell behind her knees with a brilliant karate kick so that she crumpled to the ground and fell on the Inspector's dog, which was very upset and bit her.

What with Thumper barking and sirens going off and water squirting over the garage, Mr Maxwell got into a real panic. He suddenly yelled, 'All right, all right. I admit it! I've been forging the tickets.'

Well, I can't say I was surprised. It was obvious really. It turned out that the Maxwells' shop was in trouble and he needed the money. He should give up the cigarettes, that's what I say.

But once Mr Maxwell and his wife (who was in on the scam) had been taken away, I went to speak to Inspector Crockitt.

'I have to admit you were right, Damian,' he said. 'There *was* somebody forging tickets.'

'I know,' I said. 'But this is the man who was selling them.' And I held out the photo.

Inspector Crockitt's jaw dropped. 'That's Mr Maxwell's brother,' he said.

That was a real surprise. It turned out to be a family crime. Mr Maxwell, Mrs Maxwell and the brother. Just like the Mafia and that. Amazing!

What I didn't know was that Inspector Crockitt had phoned Mum (*again!*) and she soon arrived on the scene.

I may be famous in our town but I

was in dead trouble with Mum. Did she care that I had tracked down major criminals? Did she care that I had got the police and the fire brigade to come in the nick of time?

No, she didn't.

'I'm ashamed of you, Damian,' she said. (She was in one of her moods.) 'When Inspector Crockitt rang me, I was shocked! How could you behave like that?'

I didn't know why she was so mad with me. She went on and on and practically dragged me all the way home.

But I wasn't the only one in trouble. Winston got a right earful from his dad.

He lost a week's pocket money. Even Thumper was in the doghouse because he bit Mr Maxwell's leg when he tried to run away. I believe he should have a medal.

Dixie Stanton got told off for attacking Mrs Maxwell. Inspector Crockitt said he would talk to Dixie's mum next week. I've told her not to worry as the Inspector is a friend of mine.

As for Annabelle, I gave her a box of chocolates. After all, she had taken the photograph which was quite important. But I suggested she kept quiet about it and maybe I'd let her be one of my trainee detectives.